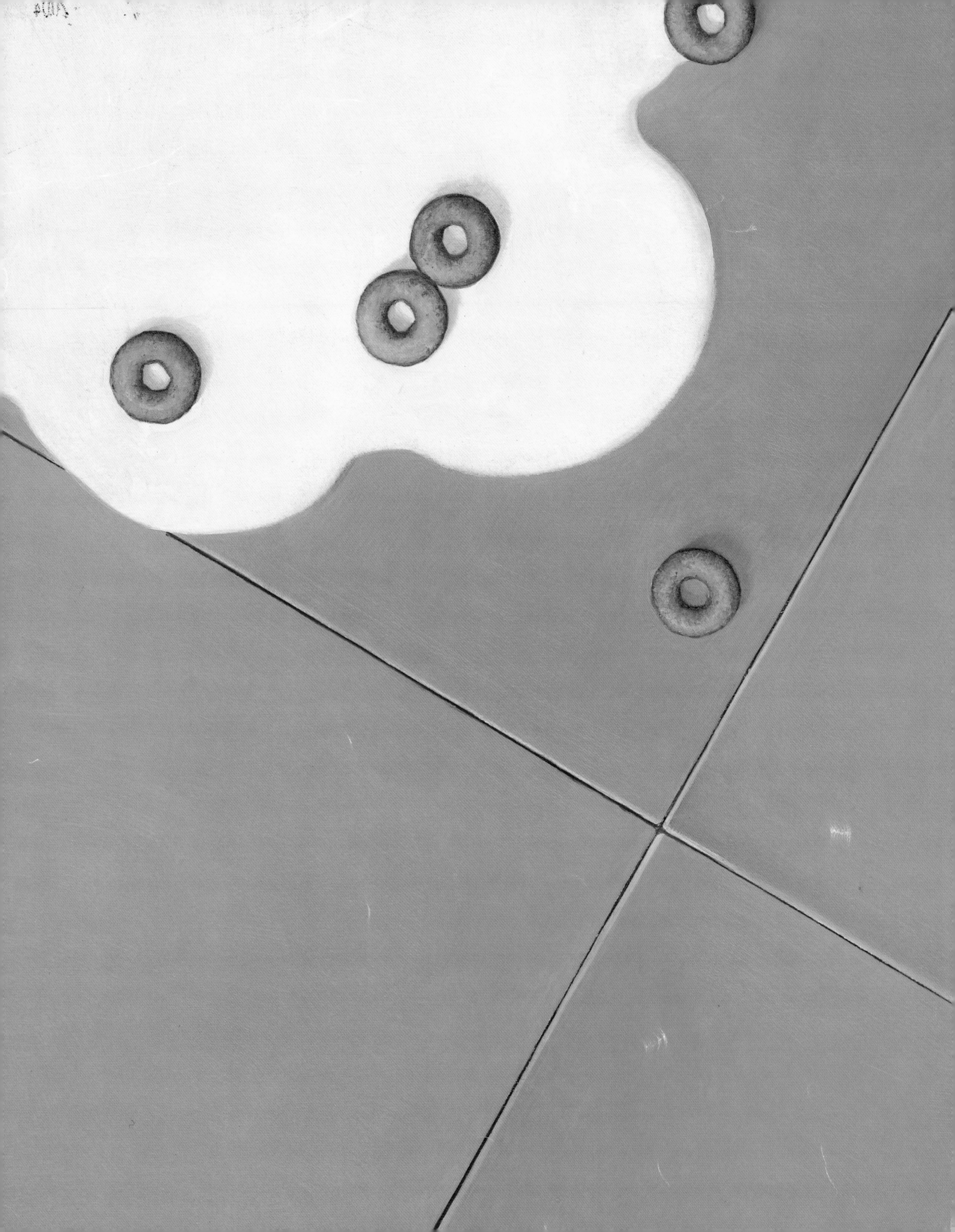

A Special Day For MOMMY

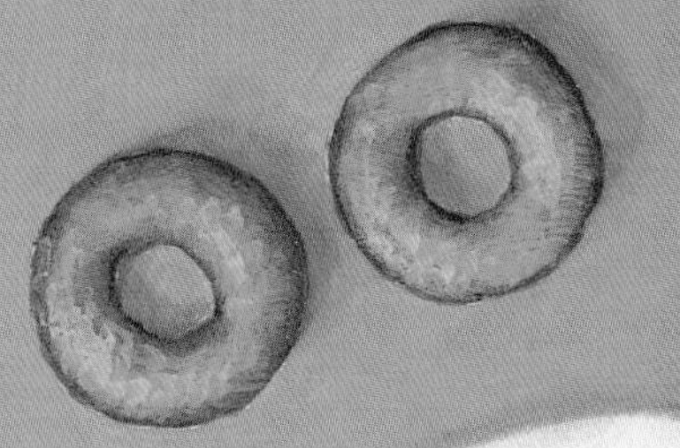

by DAN ANDREASEN

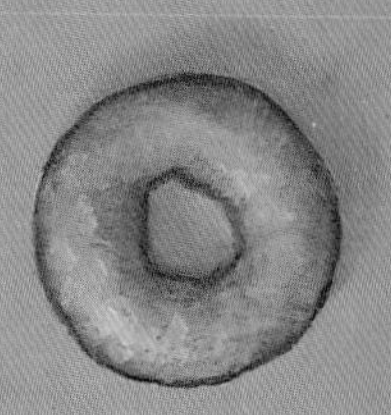

Margaret K. McElderry Books
New York London Toronto Sydney Singapore

I'm making breakfast
in bed for Mommy
because today
is her special day.

Wake up, Mommy!

Did I surprise you, Mommy?

Now I'm going to make
Mommy a card with lots of
pink hearts on it.
She will like that.

To cut out a heart that's not crooked, fold the paper in half first. No peeking, Mommy!

Mommy loves
yellow daffodils.
I know because she
planted them all
around the house.

Quick, Mommy!

I need a jar of water this big!

I know! It needs a great big bow.

There! That's perfect!

Mommy and I love jelly-butter sandwiches. I can make them all by myself.

First I spread jelly
on one slice of bread
and butter on another.
Next I smoosh them
together really hard.
I cut out fun shapes
with cookie cutters.

It’s easy!

Yuck! I'm all sticky, Mommy!

Hold my hand, and close your eyes

really tight, Mommy!

SURPRISE!

I bet
you wish
EVERY
day
was
Mommy's
special
day!

For my mother, Mary,

and my daughter, Katrina

—D. A.

Margaret K. McElderry Books
An imprint of Simon & Schuster Children's Publishing Division
1230 Avenue of the Americas, New York, New York 10020

Book design by Ann Bobco
The text for this book is set in ITC Officina Serif.
The illustrations for this book are rendered in oil paint.
Manufactured in China
2 4 6 8 10 9 7 5 3 1
Library of Congress Cataloging-in-Publication Data
Andreasen, Dan.
A special day for Mommy / Dan Andreasen.— 1st ed.
p. cm.
Summary: A little pig does her best to create a special day for her mother.
ISBN 0-689-84977-X (hardcover)
[1. Mothers and daughters—Fiction. 2. Pigs—Fiction.] I. Title.
PZ7.A55915Sp 2004
[E]—dc21
2002156427
FIRST EDITION